A Minute To Kill

Joh

Stanl

First published in 1997 by:
Stanley Thornes (Publishers) Ltd
Ellenborough House
Wellington Street
CHELTENHAM GL50 1YW
England

97 98 99 00 01 / 10 9 8 7 6 5 4 3 2 1

A catalogue record for this book is available from the British Library.

ISBN 0-7487-3086-9

Cover artwork by Paul McCaffrey
Typeset by Tech-Set, Gateshead
Printed and bound in Great Britain at Martin's The Printers, Berwick

1

The finger moved. Just a twitch – but it moved . . . for the very last time. The body was slumped over the desk. The twisted face lay on an open book. Both eyes stared up at the window in the gloomy afternoon. From his right hand, a gold pen fell to the floor with a splash of black ink.

The head turned, the throat gurgled, the mouth dribbled onto the book, the eyelids blinked and then all was still . . . very still. Nothing. The man was dead and the skin on his cheeks was already cold – like cool wax. Life had slipped away in minutes.

No longer did the heart pump blood. The pulse had now stopped. His arms hung down from the desk. The end had come quickly. The plan had worked. It had all gone like clock-work . . . the perfect murder – or so it seemed. It took no more than one minute to kill.

There were no tell-tale signs. There was no trail of blood, no finger prints, no smoking gun, no sign of a struggle, not even the slam of a door. The room was just as it had always been. Nothing had been stolen, not a pin was out of place. But he was dead all right . . . and somebody had done it. Somebody not very far away had the need to kill. Just one minute was all it took. Somebody had been waiting for this moment – and now, at last, they had struck.

My phone rang in the middle of that Saturday afternoon. At the time I was up to my ears in the compost heap and I was planning to dig the garden before the rain came. I only just heard my phone and by the time I ran to pick it up, I was out of breath. It was my cousin Jill who lived at the other end of the village.

'Hello,' I said, 'you're still in the land of the living then! I haven't seen you both for ages. What brings this little call – a war, a bomb, a fire? . . .' I could have kicked myself. I could tell something was very wrong.

'No,' she said calmly. 'It's Kevin. I've just found him in his room. He's dead.'

'What? He can't be! Not Kevin. Oh Jill, what can I say?'

She stayed very calm. 'I want you to come over quickly. I have this awful feeling that . . . he's been murdered.'

'What do the police say?' I asked.

'Nothing.'

'Nothing? Haven't they got any ideas?'

'No. I haven't told them yet. I want you to come first. I know how good you are at working things out. I know what a good detective you can be. You always solve those Miss

Marple films. Well, I want you to come over and find some clues before the police arrive. I'll phone them when you're here.'

What could I say? I'm not a detective. I'm just a chemist but I like puzzles. Jill knew I was a fan of all the old late night murder films. But this was for real. My own cousin – I couldn't believe she was saying this. Before I knew what I was doing, I said, 'Of course I will come over. I'll be with you in a few minutes.'

The next bit sounded just like one of those corny old films. 'Oh, and Jill – don't touch anything. Leave the body just as it is.'

'Don't worry,' she said, 'I'm not going back in that room alone.'

'Oh, and make sure the dog is safely locked away,' I said.

She put the phone down and I went to change out of my gardening clothes. I couldn't believe what had happened. I couldn't believe that poor Jill had asked me to help. A real murder to get my teeth into. Of course, it was all very sad. I jumped in the car and sped off through the village.

So how could I solve this puzzle? It was not as simple as it might seem. There was a lot of thinking to be done. Perhaps you can solve the crime quicker than I did! Let me tell you the story and see if you can pick up all the right clues. I will give you all the facts. You will have to make a careful note of them and try to find the murderer.

This is your first clue – it was someone in the village. I can tell you that now. Yes, one of the people I will tell you about is the killer. Your job, like mine, is to find out the truth. You must find just three answers to these three questions: Who did it? How was the murder done? Why was he killed?

Simple. Or is it? It's up to you now. I'll give you the facts. All you have to do is think about them and make up your mind. And then, it's just a matter of time – before you can point the finger . . .

2

I arrived within minutes at the Old School House, where Jill and Kevin lived. Before stepping out of the car, I looked all around to make sure Jack was safely out of the way. Jack was their dog – a huge beast that attacked anyone in trousers. He was probably named after Jack The Ripper!

Jill opened the door and hugged me. Her eyes were red and she was no longer as calm as she seemed on the phone. She was very upset.

'Thanks for coming over so quickly,' she said. 'It's good of you. I need help. Someone's got to sort this out. Kevin's body is in there. He didn't kill himself. I'm sure of that.' She pointed to his study.

'Would you like me to take a look?' I asked. She began crying.

'Just sit down and I'll make you a drink,' I said. I was sounding like some old film again. When she had calmed down, I walked slowly into Kevin's study with its white desk, blue carpet and football posters over the walls.

It was all so still. No blood, no mess, nothing out of place. Kevin was slumped at his desk, his arms hanging down and his head on one side, resting on the desk. The eyes were open and stared at the window. His face rested on a book – the local *Yellow Pages* open at the letter 'P' . . . Post Offices to Potato Farms. I placed my hand gently on his cheek – it was stone cold. There was no doubt about it, he was dead.

On the floor by his side was a gold pen with a few splashes of ink beside it on the carpet. I turned to Jill who was standing behind me at the door. 'How long has he been like this?'

'I found him only fifteen minutes ago and then I phoned you straight away. We'd been talking only half an hour before that and then I went round to the back garden to hang out some washing. I came back in to ask him if he wanted a cup of tea and there he was . . .'

She began sobbing again.

'But Jill,' I began, 'why on earth did you call *me*? You must call the police. You said he had been murdered. It doesn't look that way to me. His heart must have given out. He must have blacked out and died.' Even as I said it, I knew it was a stupid thing to say. Kevin was a fitness freak. He jogged everywhere with Jack running along beside him. He was only in his thirties – surely he couldn't just pass out sitting at his desk.

'No,' Jill said calmly. 'No, there's more to it than that. There's something else. Something I didn't tell you about. Look.'

She was pointing to a scrap of paper on the desk. It was almost hidden by Kevin's right shoulder. I picked it up.

There were just three words written on it in Kevin's handwriting. There was no doubt that it was his writing – big letters with odd loops. It had been written in black ink with the pen that lay on the floor. The three words stood out large and clear – CAN'T GO ON. 'So . . . he took his own life. Oh Jill, I'm so sorry. I had no idea it was like this. I didn't know he was so unhappy.'

I couldn't work out why she had called me over. It was a clear case of suicide and here was the proof.

'Oh no,' Jill said. 'A heart attack I might just begin to believe but he did not kill himself. Never in a million years would he do that. I know him. We were married for ten years. Kevin may have written that note but he did not kill himself. I know it. I think he was made to write it. That's why I'm sure it's murder.'

'We'll need more proof,' I said. 'Even if you're right, we'll have to find real proof.'

'That's why I called you. If anyone can sort this out, you can. The police won't understand. They will read that note and say it was suicide. But I'm telling you straight – Kevin did not just kill himself. You knew him. You must agree he just wouldn't do it. He had everything to live for. You see . . . I'm expecting our baby. He was over the moon and . . .' She began to cry.

I had to agree with her. It did look odd. There he was, just slumped over his desk with one little note to the world saying he couldn't go on. She was so sure it was murder and she was begging me to help her. As I stood there in his study on that gloomy afternoon, looking down at Kevin's body, I knew she was right. In fact there was no doubt about it. I was sure that this was a case of murder.

3

The rain swept across the fields from the west. Grey clouds hung low over the village. I looked out through Kevin's window as the rain ran down the glass and I thought about the man who now lay dead beside me. Who would want to kill him? How had he died? And why?

We hadn't really thought about that. There he was, slumped over the desk and we hadn't talked about the way he died. I could see no marks on the skin, no bump or bruise. Healthy men don't just die. And why did he write a note saying 'CAN'T GO ON?' There was no sign of a break-in, no footprint in the flower bed, no broken window pane, no forced door. It was looking more and more like suicide. How could he be murdered in broad daylight in his own home with his wife hanging out the washing in the garden and a big dog on the loose?

That was odd. The rain was now beating against the glass. A few minutes ago I had been digging my garden and thinking about calling it a day because of the bad weather. But Jill said she was hanging out the washing. I turned and looked her straight in the eyes. 'Not a very nice day for the washing,' I said. She glared at me.

'I called you to help me – not to make sick jokes.'

I decided to ask her straight and see how she acted. 'You weren't doing the washing at all, were you? That washing machine is as dry as a bone and no one would hang out sheets in this weather.'

She said nothing. She just stared at me.

'You've got to be honest with me, Jill – if I'm going to help. No lies.'

'All right,' she started, 'all right, I lied. But don't tell the police. Kevin and I had a big row. It all seems so silly now. I said something horrible to him and stormed out. I walked up the lane to calm down. I was back in half an hour – after I had cooled down a bit. I came back in here to say I was sorry . . . and there he was. He was dead. But really, we often had little rows like that. It was no reason to get upset and . . . and . . .'

'And to kill himself?' I finished her sentence for her.

'No,' she said. 'It was nothing. I tell you, I knew Kevin so well. He would never take his own life.'

I looked at her straight in the eyes again. 'No, maybe not,' I said. 'But what about YOU? You might have killed him.' I half expected her to hit me.

'I know that's what some people might think,' she began, 'but I didn't. I promise you that. I give you my word.'

She began to cry and I really believed her. She would never harm anyone, let alone Kevin. I could see why she needed help to make the police see he was killed by someone. But who and how? What clues could I look for?

Perhaps the *Yellow Pages* on the desk was a clue. Could Kevin have been trying to find a number when he died? Was he trying to tell us something? But there were hundreds of numbers on those pages . . . Post Offices and Potato Farms. What help could they be?

Suddenly there was a blood-curdling howl from the back of the house. I sprang to my feet.

'It's all right, it's only Jack wanting his tea,' Jill said.

'Well don't let him out while I'm here or I'll be his tea! You know what happened last time.' I still have the scars.

'Has Jack been locked away all day?' I asked.

'Oh no. He's been on the loose all day. I only put him in the back room when you came.'

So how could anyone have broken in to kill Kevin? Jack would attack anyone in trousers and never let go. Unless, of course, the murderer had been a woman. Jack didn't seem to mind women so much. I looked back at the open *Yellow Pages* on the desk and it was then that I had the idea . . .

4

Across the road from the Old School House where Kevin and Jill lived, Miss Knight kept the village post office and shop. She was a strange dumpy little woman with sharp grey eyes. Many of the local children thought she was a witch and wouldn't go in her shop. She seemed to know too much about everybody and made us all feel uneasy.

The bell rang when I pushed open the door. At once her eyes were on me, fixing me in their powerful stare. She always seemed to know just what I was thinking. Nothing happened in our village without Miss Knight knowing all about it. She never smiled.

If anybody had seen a murder in our village, it would be Miss Knight. As it was Saturday afternoon, the post office part of her shop was closed. She was filling shelves with soap and just carried on as if I was not there.

'Something wrong?' she said in her squeaky witch's voice. Her chin had more whiskers than a pet shop.

'Not really,' I said, trying to sound calm and not wanting to give anything away. She stared up at me with a knowing look – like a school teacher catching you cheating in maths. She had always looked at me like that, ever since I moved into the village three years ago.

'Ah,' she began, 'so everything is fine over there, is it?' She looked over the road at the house. Her grey eyes were fixed on the window to Kevin's study. I felt sure this woman knew something and a shiver ran down my back. She gave me the creeps.

'How do you mean?' I asked.

'I just keep my eyes open, that's all. Now then, dear, what can I do for you?'

'Er . . . a chocolate bar, please.' There was almost the start of a smile on her face. She knew very well that I hadn't gone in for a chocolate bar.

'You see, dear, I saw you rush into their drive just now. It looked rather urgent to me.'

'I see,' I said. 'Have you seen anything else by any chance?'

'Like what?'

'Like Kevin. How is he these days?'

She just stared at me – a long, cold, hard stare. Those sharp grey eyes drilled into mine. She knew something.

'Have you seen him lately?' I asked, trying to sound cool and calm.

'Yes. Just now. You look surprised, dear.'

'Do I?'

'Is he feeling any better?'

There was something about this woman I didn't like. She sensed something and looked at me as if she knew just what had happened. That gloomy little shop grew darker as the rain poured down outside.

'What makes you think Kevin is ill?' I asked.

'I can tell. He didn't look too good just now when he posted his letter.'

'Posted a letter? When?'

'About half an hour ago. He went back indoors very fast just before his wife came back. A little row, I expect.'

'Has the postman collected the letters from the post-box yet?'

'Oh no – not till Monday morning now.'

'What? Not till Monday? That's two days!'

Her lips curled into a sly grin. 'A long time for such an important letter to stay there alone in the box. Don't you think? It might need looking after.'

My mind was now hard at work trying to sort it all out. She must have been one of the last people to see Kevin alive. 'Was Jack with him?'

'The dog? Well of course. Better safe than sorry, eh?' She gave me another of her knowing looks and began dusting the counter. What did she mean?

'What on earth do you mean by that?' I shouted at her.

'Maybe you ought to ask the police.'

'Police? What have they got to do with it? Tell me, what do you know? What have you seen? What do you know about the police?'

'Just ask them. Look, there they are. Over the road. They've arrived.'

A police car drove into the drive and parked next to my car. She leaned forward on the counter and gazed straight into my eyes. 'I hope they leave enough room.' I had no idea what she meant.

'What do you mean?' I was puzzled.

'For the ambulance, of course.'

She really gave me the creeps now. I turned and left the shop and the creepy little woman inside. I left the jangling bell behind me, and the chocolate bar on the counter. But that was the least of my worries. Just as I got to the front door of the house, the ambulance arrived.

5

Jill had called the police while I was in the post office. It didn't take them long to arrive and start asking all their questions. They took photographs, our finger prints and looked all through the house. Only when they had made hundreds of notes did they let the ambulance take the body away. A police woman spent a long time talking with Jill and gave her another shoulder to cry on.

They asked what I was doing there, but we didn't say anything about me looking for clues or trying to solve the murder. In fact, they didn't seem too worried about it all. They were all very calm. Perhaps they see murders every day of the week. Perhaps they didn't think it was murder.

They took some photographs of Kevin at his desk and looked in his ears, eyes and mouth, then they put his body onto a stretcher. He was covered with a blanket and taken away. That was the last I saw of him. It all seemed so normal to the police. Just another body to be taken away.

The news spread through the village in seconds. A crowd stood outside as the ambulance drove away. There, at the window of her post office, was Miss Knight, staring at all of us.

The police were very interested in Kevin's note saying 'CAN'T GO ON'. They matched it with other pages of his writing and took it away for tests. They took his pen as well. His body was to have a post mortem to find out just how and when he died. At last the police left and I tried to comfort Jill. She was feeling even more upset after all those questions. She felt sure they thought Kevin had killed himself.

I hadn't told her about Kevin posting that letter just minutes before he died – but I kept it very much in my mind. That letter could be a key to unlock all this. There was a question the police had asked but I wanted to know more.

'Jill, did Kevin have any enemies? I mean, can you think of anyone at all who would want him out the way? Did he ever tell you about anyone?'

'No,' she said. 'That's what I keep asking myself. Who would want to do this? I know he was no angel and he upset a few people from time to time but he had no real enemies. He got into the odd row at the pub now and again and upset a few people – but nothing to cause this.'

I had to ask the next question. 'What about you? Did he leave a will?' She told me she would get a lot of money from the insurance so she would not be hard up. I asked her if Kevin had been on edge lately. Had he been worried?

'No more than usual. I mean, he's always been a bit careful about being safe. For over a year he's been fussy about locking doors and things. He always checked under his car and had alarms fitted. In fact, I think that's why he got Jack – to look after him. He never said anything to me but maybe he was scared of someone. As if he knew he might be in danger . . .'

I held her hand. 'Listen, Jill, if I am going to help you, I need to know everything. The police will be back to ask more questions and look at all his private things. Don't you think I ought to take a look first – just in case there are some clues?'

She sat and thought for a while. 'Well there's nothing really. You can look up in the loft if you like, in his boxes. Everything else is locked in his private drawer in his study but I've no idea where he kept the key.'

I went to that drawer and tried to open it but it was locked tight. 'Try to think,' I said. 'This could be important. I need to look in that drawer before the police come again.' It was no good. She had no idea where the key was.

I changed the subject. 'I know it's not easy, but we'll need to think about the funeral and things. We must make plans. There will be a lot of paper work but I can help with that.'

'I've already thought of that,' she said. 'I phoned the vicar and he said he would come round to see me this evening.

Would you stay and see him with me?' I was happy to help. The vicar knew me quite well and he knew Kevin. We once did some building work for him on the church wall.

The vicar arrived fairly soon and began by giving Jill such a hug that she cried again. I poured us all some strong drinks. He said he had only been bell-ringing with Kevin the night before and he was as upset as the rest of us. I then went out into the kitchen to make some coffee and left the two of them to talk. I thought I would have another quick look around Kevin's study.

I slowly pushed the door open and peered around inside. It was so still and cold and dark. I switched on the desk lamp and tried to force open the drawer. The only sound was the clock ticking on the wall. I was just thinking about the deathly hush after all the clatter the police had made when I was suddenly startled by a tapping sound. It came from the window.

When I turned, I saw a dirty hand clawing outside at the glass. It looked like there were splashes of black ink on the fingers. In a mad panic, I switched off the desk lamp and saw a pale face with two staring eyes. It disappeared into the darkness and melted into the night.

I'm not sure if I screamed. All I know is, I ran from the room in a blind panic. I was in a cold sweat and my hands shook. Was Kevin trying to come back? Was this some kind of ghost trying to get back into the room? By the time I got outside, dreading what I might find, there was nobody there. Not a sign. The night was still.

I turned round and walked back into the house towards the back room. This was the time to let the dog out on the loose.

6

In no time at all, the dog had run all round the garden. There was no one out there. Where was that face I had seen so clearly at the window? All the dog found was a rabbit in the bushes while I looked all round the house. Someone had tapped on that window and I couldn't rest until I found out who had done it. Meanwhile, Jill had taken the dog back indoors and into the sitting room. Even the thought of his snarling teeth didn't stop me going back in!

The dog growled when I walked into the room. Jill and the vicar were still talking and making plans for the funeral. For some reason, the dog didn't growl at him. In fact, once or twice the vicar patted Jack on the head without so much as a tooth showing in anger. That rather surprised me. What faith!

The police had looked through all the bedrooms, dusted for finger prints, asked what Kevin had for breakfast and maybe they even asked if he liked salt or ketchup on his chips. What could they have looked for upstairs? I went up and had a look around. In one of Kevin's pockets I found what I was after. It was a small key. I went back into his study to try the key in the lock of his desk drawer.

I stood in Kevin's room again. By now he must be lying on a slab somewhere so the police could open him up for tests and reports. I looked up at the window where the face had been. Twigs scratched at the glass like cat's claws. The key clicked in the lock and the drawer slid open.

Inside were all kinds of papers and folders. I put them all in a bag and took them upstairs to the spare bedroom. I would look at them later. Jill had asked me to spend the next few nights at the house as she was too upset to stay there alone.

After an hour or so, the vicar left. As we stood at the door to see him go, Jill smiled for the first time. 'Why are you smiling?' I asked.

'Your mystery face at the window,' she said. 'It was Ron. He doesn't know the news yet. He always leaves a sack of spuds by Kevin's window. Look.'

She was right. There was a sack of potatoes leaning against the wall outside Kevin's room. She shone her torch onto the shadow which looked like a body slumped under the window sill. The twigs still scratched at the glass like twisted fingers. I must have been staring in a daze till Jill's hand touched my arm. 'You know – Ron and Penny . . .'

Ron Bates and his wife lived at the farm across the field from the Old School House. I knew them fairly well.

'Then maybe I ought to pop over and see them and let them know,' I said. I remembered the open *Yellow Pages* by

Kevin's body. As well as Post Offices, it also had Potato Farms listed. I thought of Ron and his potatoes. Could it be a clue? I went back and found the page. Sure enough, on the page that had been open, there was the name . . . R. Bates. Had Kevin been trying to tell us something in his last few seconds alive?

Jill said she wanted some time alone to sort herself out, to make some plans and to phone the family. I walked along the lane towards the Bates' farm at about nine o'clock. The moon gave enough light for me to see the track leading up to their farm. I kept thinking about the post-box and Kevin's last letter which he posted minutes before his death. I knew I would not rest till I got it out of the post-box. That letter could point the finger to the killer.

Ron Bates said it was his face at Kevin's window and he had no idea about the news. I looked at his hands which were black with grease. Ron was stunned when I told him about Kevin but Penny, his wife, showed no sign of shock. She just said, 'Well now maybe that dog of his will be kept away from here. He was always letting it run loose on our land – always scaring my cats and upsetting the sheep.' She was mad about cats and she had no time for Kevin and his dog. 'I hate the man. Ever since he shot at my cat when he was after rabbits.'

'Penny, Kevin is dead. Show some respect.' Her husband tried to calm her down.

'I believe in speaking my mind,' she went on. 'I never did like that man. Always boozing. He was up to something if you ask me. That Jill is a funny sort, too.' She sat stroking one of her cats on her lap.

Ron spoke next. 'He was all right really. It's just that we had a row a few months back. It was about some rat poison I put down in one of the barns. I'm always careful with poison – because of her cats – but one day his dog got in and was sniffing at it. Kevin got very angry with me. The idea of poison seemed to get him all worked up and upset. Just as if . . .' He stopped himself.

'I see,' I said. That word 'POISON' ran through my mind and started me thinking.

As I walked back along the lane, I couldn't help feeling puzzled by these two. There was something odd about them. I remembered how Ron once asked me if I could get him a bottle of strong poison from my lab at work. He said it was to kill foxes but I told him 'no'. I could lose my job.

I turned into Jill's drive and saw the lights at the sitting room window. An orange glow spilled out through the curtains into the night. It was then that I saw a strange shadow by my car. Someone was peering into the car window.

7

I stood in the darkness and waited for the person to speak.
The eyes looked up at me and I knew at once it was the
strange Miss Knight from the post office over the road.
'Yes?' I said sharply. 'What do you want?'

'Just bringing over your chocolate bar, dear. You left it in my
shop. Just looking at that car of yours. So sad about Kevin.
Killed in his own room. Just minutes after I saw him. So
pale, too. Two murders in three years. They never did find
that school-girl, did they? Killed in the lane. Poor Sally.
What a sad village we live in. And they say bad news
comes in threes. So who will be the next, do you think?'

She crept away and mumbled to herself, leaving me staring at
her shadow. An icy shiver ran down my spine. The chocolate
bar was pinned under my windscreen wiper. Why had she
waited till now? Who had told her it was murder?

The next morning brought many callers to the house.
People in the village came to see Jill. They brought cards
and flowers. So far, she was taking Kevin's death quite well,
but she would often sit in his chair at the desk and gaze out
of his window in deep thought.

Half-way through Sunday morning, P.C. Ford called round.
He lived only a few houses away from me at the other end of

the village and I often saw him in the local pub. He was well-known in the village and was liked by us all. Kevin often went fishing with him, so he was quite upset to hear the news. Jill spoke with him for some time and then he said to me, 'If there's anything I can do to help, just let me know.'

'Thanks,' I said. 'Have you heard anything yet? Do they know how he died?'

'Well, I'm not supposed to say anything yet but it was poison. No doubt about that. A very strong and deadly type. Only a drop and it kills in minutes.'

'Could someone have put it in his tea or something?' I asked.

'No. He hadn't drunk anything for hours. Nor eaten. The stomach was almost empty. That's why it killed him so fast. If you ask me, he got hold of a pill from somewhere, just popped it in and wrote that note. Very sad. I had no idea he felt so down in the dumps. It's her I feel sorry for. You know what this place is like for gossip.'

'Are they sure it's not one of those darts with a poison tip?' I asked.

'You've been watching too many Tarzan films. No, it was in the stomach. A tiny drop is all it takes. Don't say anything about it to Jill but we feel sure it's suicide. Some more of our chaps will be over again today to do a few more tests and things but they don't smell a rat. Nothing's odd about this one. No one is making a fuss. Things just got on top of poor old Kevin, that's all.'

By midday Jill took the phone off the hook. So many people kept phoning and all she wanted was rest. A newspaper got wind of the story and wanted to talk to her. We shut ourselves away in the sitting room. But any thoughts of a quiet afternoon were suddenly shattered with the arrival of Kevin's sister, Julie. Her new red Fiesta screeched to a halt next to my car and she swept into the house like a whirl-wind, ready to take charge. She and Jill had never got on. When they met there was always a row.

Julie knew a lot about horses and was always betting on them. She spent all her winnings on fur coats or on another new car. Kevin used to say she changed her car more often than her tights! She had come over to go through all Kevin's things and to take them away with her. We didn't let her and that made for another row. At last she went and booked a room at the pub for the next few nights. She roared off in her shiny Fiesta and we didn't see her again till the funeral.

I was already pleased with the way things were going. I felt I had done my part of the job well and it was only a matter of time before the last bit was in place. I would soon clear this one up! The only problem now was what to do with that letter sitting out there in the post-box.

Jill told me that Kevin got a letter just before he died. She said it looked like junk mail – one of those ways to win a fortune. It could have been his football coupons or scratch cards. There was a paper clip and a form to fill in. She thought Kevin filled it in and he probably sent it back straight away.

I needed to get hold of that letter. That creepy Miss Knight knew about it too. Oh yes, she knew all right. If she got her hands on it, who could tell what would happen? The police would want to see it as well. But I needed that letter first. I just had to find a way to get it back. It was a job I was keeping for the dead of night . . .

8

It was two o'clock on Monday morning when I crept over to the
post-box. That letter was still inside – the one Kevin posted
just a minute before his death. I had to get it before morning,
when the box would be emptied. I gently eased my hand
inside but there was no way my arm would reach. I nearly got
stuck. I could just imagine what Miss Knight would say if I
had to wake her up and ask if I could have my arm back!

The owls were screeching up in the trees and a fox ran
through the bushes at the side of the road. Somewhere
across the fields a dog howled and the chilling sound was
carried through the night. I held my breath and groped
inside the post-box. My hand touched something smooth. I
gripped it with my fingers and pulled it out. I jumped at the
sight of the slug squelching in my hand!

I had a plan to get Kevin's letter but my plan depended on
two things. Number one – a paper clip had to be inside the
envelope. Number two – Kevin's letter had to be on top of
the pile.

I had a magnet on a bit of string. Slowly I let it down inside
the post-box . . . and hoped for a bite. Nothing. Every time I
pulled back the string, there was no letter on the magnet. I
tried again and again with the magnet clattering around
inside the post-box.

Suddenly a light flashed on. I looked up and saw a glow at Miss Knight's window. I ducked down in the shadows. What would be worse – her seeing me with my hand in the post-box, or me seeing her in her nightie? When at last the light went off again, I carried on with my 'fishing'.

At last I pulled out a letter. It was a long brown envelope with a printed address on it – some P.O. Box Number in Bedford. I could feel two paper clips inside. This was it. This was what I was looking for. I would take it back to my room and take a look inside.

Turning away from the post-box, I suddenly found myself face to face with two grey eyes. 'Good evening, Miss Knight,' I said. 'Nice evening. Don't catch cold, will you? Just posting my cards early for Christmas!'

I crossed the road. She said nothing but just stood there with her mouth open, staring at me as I walked back to the front door and let myself indoors.

Once upstairs in the spare room, I opened the envelope. Yes, I held it in my hand – none other than . . . the murder weapon! Inside was a typed letter to Kevin and pinned to it was a number – a lucky number. This is what the letter said:

Well done! You have been chosen from millions to be lucky! You could win £1,000,000 in our Prize Draw.

Your name has been entered with the name of a lucky horse. All you have to do is sign this letter and send it back to us straight away in the envelope. Make a note of YOUR lucky horse on a piece of paper and keep it safe. It is called 'CAN'T GO ON'. Return this letter now for your chance to win a million. Just stick the enclosed stamp onto the envelope, seal it down and post NOW. Pin your lucky number to this letter and wait for your fortune to arrive. Good Luck!

So Kevin thought he was entering a draw. He hoped to win a prize with a lucky horse and number. But it wasn't very lucky – that letter had killed him. The killer knew the victim would hide the murder weapon himself by posting it out of sight.

The poison had been coated on the back of the stamp and on the flap of the envelope. A few licks was all it took. Deadly poison. Murder by post. Kevin had licked the envelope, walked over the road to post the letter and by the time he got back to his room, he was dying. The killer had not even set foot in the house. The dog had no need to bark.

All so clever. Kevin must have known something was odd about that letter as he was dying, so he tried to use the *Yellow Pages* and phone the post office just over the road. He was trying to phone Miss Knight to tell her to keep hold of that envelope – the murder weapon. But he dropped dead before he had the chance. He was about to write a note but he slumped forward and the pen fell from his hand.

It took just a minute to kill. A minute to die. So that is how it was done. Did you guess? Did you work it out? Next time you lick a stamp or an envelope, you might think twice!

But now you need to ask another question. You know HOW Kevin was killed. Do you know WHY? There must have been a reason. Nobody kills another person without a proper reason . . . do they? I bet you'll never guess the reason WHY.

9

The funeral was held a few days later. I told no one about the poison and the letter – not yet. I put it with the papers I had found in Kevin's drawer and warned Jill that if anything should happen to me, she must look after that bag of papers. There were secrets inside.

The police, the people in the village and the newspapers still thought Kevin had killed himself. A headline in our local paper read 'Man Takes His Own Life.' That upset Jill a lot.

She coped very well at the funeral. The village church was almost full with Kevin's family, people from the village and from where he worked.

The April sun shone down on the daffodils in the graveyard where we stood round Kevin's grave. We all looked silently down at the hole dug at our feet. A gun shot rang out from across the fields and above us the birds flew from the tree tops. Their cries were carried away on the wind as the vicar said a prayer at the graveside.

Most of the people there felt sorry for Jill. She was the one who had to go on living in that house. How sad for the wife when a man kills himself. But I knew that Kevin's killer was standing there with us at the funeral. It would only be a matter of time before I would tell what I knew.

We looked around at all the faces. The vicar and his wife stood at one end of the group, next to Bill Green who worked at the local garage. He and Kevin had grown up together. I stood next to the village doctor who had also known Kevin for many years.

Julie wore a black silk dress and cried most of the time. She was looked after by P.C. Ford who held her arm. Also standing arm in arm were Penny and Ron Bates from the farm. She wore dark glasses and smelt of brandy. Standing a little way apart from the rest of us was Miss Knight, who seemed to be watching me all through the service. Those sharp grey eyes were either fixed on me or on the coffin.

There was also another woman there. She stood on her own some way off. We all knew her as the mother of the missing school-girl from our village. The one who had never been found. It reminded us all of the sad events in the village over the last three years. Death, it seemed, had struck twice. And it was all because of one person. That person was standing there that morning in the churchyard under the warm April sun.

10

So now you know most of the facts. I know more than the police, who will never sort this out now unless I help them. They are still happy to call Kevin's case SUICIDE. But I expect you want to find out some more. Perhaps you will pick the killer if I tell you *why* Kevin was killed.

I found what I was looking for in Kevin's locked drawer. There were many newspaper cuttings from three years ago. They were all about that shocking story in our village. A girl of fifteen just disappeared into thin air and was never found. She went out one evening to see her friend in the next village, but she was never seen again.

Kevin had kept all the details in his drawer. He also had letters. They had been written to him – from the girl's murderer. Yes, she had been killed and Kevin knew who killed her. The letters showed that Kevin had been blackmailing someone. He had known all about the missing girl.

Those letters told the story. Kevin had been out shooting rabbits one evening. It was the night the girl went missing. He had seen it all from the hill. He had a clear view of the bend in the lane – and of Sally walking her dog. The red sports car roared round the corner, but the driver was drunk and the car went out of control. It hit the girl head-on. She stood no chance. In a mad panic, the driver got out of the car and bundled the girl into the back. She was dead.

The driver later hid the body. It couldn't be left by the road. The car was dented and its red paint was on the girl's dress. If the police traced the driver, it could mean prison. It would be spread over all the papers. Everyone in the village would know what happened. The shame would be too much. The girl's body was buried in the driver's garden.

She is still there today and nobody knows. But Kevin knew. He warned that he would tell the girl's mother the truth . . . unless the driver paid up – every month. Every first Monday on the dot. If the money wasn't paid, he would not keep quiet. The whole village would get to hear about the night the girl disappeared. But the blackmail letters became too much of a worry. The killer got fed up. Fed up with the blackmail letters. Fed up with paying.

Only Kevin knew about the killer and the dark secret. But now the time had come to get rid of Kevin. He had become too greedy. Yes, the driver of that car was also Kevin's murderer.

So now to the big question. Who was it? Of course, I'm not just going to tell you the answer. Not after going to all the trouble of keeping you guessing. You've got to do a little more looking yet. There is a secret message hidden in this book. After all, you could have cheated. So many people flick to the last page to find out the answer before they read all the facts. Well, it's not going to be quite that easy. There is some more work to do yet. I wonder if anyone is as clever as I have been. Will you get it right?

To find out who the killer is, you have to turn back to page *twenty four* and the start of chapter six. Look at the first paragraph. Now take the first letter from the start of each sentence. Put them together and it will spell a message. There are seven letters in all and they make three words. Just three short words. Can you guess what they say?

A two letter word, then a three letter word, then another two letter word. All very simple. So now you know. It all makes sense, doesn't it?

Not bad. You've done it. Don't you think it's clever? Don't you think I've been pretty smart? I do. There'll be no more money to pay out every month now. No more worries. It couldn't have gone better! Did you guess right? Not a soul knows!

I hope you won't tell anyone. Don't let on to the police. And Jill will never know the truth. Not now. Not if we keep it to ourselves. After all, it's our little secret. A special secret – just between you and me . . . and no one else . . . unless you count my compost heap . . .